Washing-up Will

Maverick
Early Readers

'Washing-up Will'
An original concept by Jenny Moore
© Jenny Moore

Illustrated by Floss Pottage

Published by MAVERICK ARTS PUBLISHING LTD
Studio 11, City Business Centre, 6 Brighton Road,
Horsham, West Sussex, RH13 5BB
© Maverick Arts Publishing Limited November 2020
+44 (0)1403 256941

A CIP catalogue record for this book is available at the British Library.

ISBN 978-1-84886-722-2

www.maverickbooks.co.uk

This book is rated as: Gold Band (Guided Reading)

Washing-up Will

By Jenny Moore   Illustrated by
                        Floss Pottage

Chapter 1

Will the washing-up fairy had been looking forward to watching 'Baking Magic' all day. But as soon as he turned on the television, his phone rang.

Tring tring! Tring tring!

"Oh bother," grumbled Will. "I hope it's a wrong number." But it wasn't. It was his bossy boss, Mrs Sparkle, ringing with a job for him.

"I'm sending you to help the Beck family," said Mrs Sparkle. "Their dirty dishes are getting out of control."

"Okay," Will agreed. "Can I finish watching my baking show first? They're making biscuits and fairy cakes tonight."

Mrs Sparkle snorted. "Baking shows? Fairy cakes? Ridiculous! You're a washing-up fairy, not a cooking fairy. Off you go now. The Becks have just gone to bed, so be quiet. We don't want them seeing you. And no dropping the dishes this time, or there'll be trouble."

Will switched off the television with a sigh.

Not more washing-up! What if the soapy suds made his fingers slippery again? What if he smashed another cup? What if he cracked another plate? Why couldn't he be a cooking fairy instead?

Chapter 2

The Beck family lived in a big pink house at the end of a long road. Will could hear loud snoring coming from upstairs as he flew in through the cat flap.

The kitchen was in a terrible mess. Will had never seen so many dirty dishes. There were dirty knives and forks sitting on dirty plates. There were dirty spoons resting in dirty bowls.

There were splashes of tomato sauce on the walls and lumps of macaroni cheese stuck to the floor. There were even spots of chocolate icing on the teapot.

Will pulled on his yellow rubber gloves and flew across to the sink. Oh dear. It was full of muddy shoes and boots! How could he wash up in that?

"This calls for a bit of fairy magic," he said, waving his yellow fingers over the sink.

"Come on boots, out you get, it's not your turn for washing yet. **Ow!**" A filthy football boot banged into Will's knee. "**Ouch!**" A tatty trainer bumped him on the head. "**Oof!**" A wet welly smacked him on the nose.

At last the sink was clear. Will filled it with hot water and bubbles and got to work.

"Be careful," he reminded himself. "No dropping. No smashing. No cracking. Otherwise there'll be trouble. **BIG** trouble."

Chapter 3

He rubbed the mugs and glasses until they gleamed. He scrubbed the plates and bowls until they shone. He scraped the pots and pans until they sparkled. Even with fairy magic in his fingers it was hard work.

"At least I haven't broken anything yet," he said. "I must be getting better."

Will wiped sauce off the walls.

He peeled macaroni cheese off the floor.
He picked runaway raisins out of the
cat's fur.

He was just cleaning chocolate icing off
the teapot when he spotted something:
Mrs Beck's cookbook!

"One Hundred Recipes for Terrible Cooks," Will read. "Hmm. I wonder if there's a recipe for fairy cakes in here?"

He opened the cover, knocking the teapot onto the floor with a giant CRASH.

"Oh no," said Will, looking at the broken bits of china. "Not again!"

"What was that noise?" came a loud shout. Will heard heavy footsteps clomping down the stairs. Clomp, clomp, clomp.

"Oh dear," said Will. "Oh dear, oh dear, oh dear. What will Mrs Sparkle say when she finds out?"

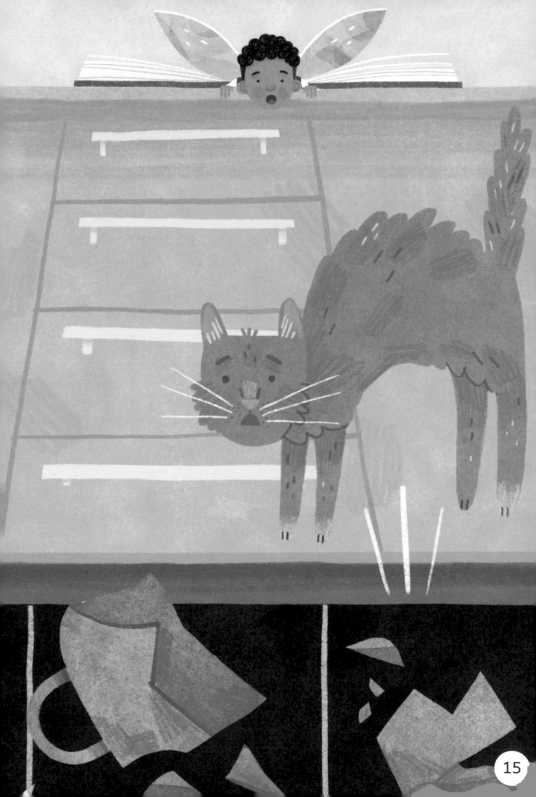

He zoomed back through the cat flap before
anyone spotted him. But he could hear Mrs
Beck crying in the kitchen.

"Oh no, not my teapot," she sobbed. "That
was a present from my aunty."
Will felt terrible. He wanted to say sorry,
but washing-up fairies were supposed to
work in secret. He couldn't let the Becks see
him or Mrs Sparkle would be even crosser.

Will flew home and went straight to bed. He wasn't in the mood for baking shows anymore. But he couldn't sleep. He still felt bad about the broken teapot.

If only there was another way of showing how sorry he was. A secret way.

That's when he had his brilliant idea.

Chapter 4

Will could hear snoring from upstairs as he flew in through the Becks' cat flap.

Mr and Mrs Beck must have swept up the bits of broken teapot and gone back to bed.

But they'd forgotten to tidy up the cookbook.

"Perfect!" said Will.

He fetched a nice clean bowl from the cupboard and a freshly washed wooden spoon.

He collected flour, sugar, butter and eggs.

Will hummed happily as he stirred and whisked. He tipped the mixture into fairy cake cases and popped them in the oven to cook.

They smelt delicious!

Will drizzled the finished fairy cakes with icing and rainbow sprinkles, singing to himself as he worked.

He was so busy singing, he didn't notice the snoring sound had stopped. He didn't hear the footsteps clomping down the stairs. He didn't hear the kitchen door creaking open...

"Who are you?" asked Mrs Beck.

"What are you doing in our kitchen?" demanded Mr Beck.

"Ooh, fairy cakes," said the Beck twins. "Can we have one?"

Will's lip trembled. His fairy knees began to knock. "I'm Will, the washing-up fairy," he said. "Mrs Sparkle sent me to help with your dirty dishes, but I broke your teapot by

mistake. I was making you some cakes to say sorry."

"A washing-up fairy?" repeated Mrs Beck, looking confused.

"Who's Mrs Sparkle?" said Mr Beck, looking dazed.

"What flavour icing is that?" asked the twins, looking hungry.

Chapter 5

It was almost time for 'Baking Magic'. But
Will the washing-up fairy was too worried to
watch television. What would Mrs Sparkle
say when she heard about the teapot?
What would she say when she discovered
he'd been spotted?

Tring tring! Tring tring!

"Oh no," said Will. "I hope it's a wrong
number." But it wasn't.

"Hello," boomed
the bossy voice at
the other end of
the line. "It's Mrs
Sparkle here."

Will's tummy grew tight.
His fairy teeth began to chatter.
"I suppose you've heard about Mrs Beck's
teapot," he said. "I didn't mean to break it.
And I didn't mean for the Becks to catch me
in their kitchen. I'm really sorry. I must be
the world's worst washing-up fairy. But it
won't happen again, I promise."

"No," agreed Mrs Sparkle. "You're right, it
won't happen again. No more washing-up for

you. You'll have to find a new job instead..."

Poor Will didn't know what to say. What would he do now?

But Mrs Sparkle hadn't finished yet.

"...And I know just the thing," she added. "The Beck family said your fairy cakes were the nicest they'd ever tasted. They'd like you to come and work for them as a cooking fairy instead. If you do the cooking and baking, they'll do the washing-up afterwards. How does that sound?"

"It sounds brilliant!" said Will. "Thanks, Mrs Sparkle."

Will the cooking fairy said goodbye and settled back into his armchair with a big grin on his face. "Time for some 'Baking Magic'," he said, switching on the television.

The End

Book Bands for Guided Reading

The Institute of Education book banding system is a scale of colours that reflects the various levels of reading difficulty. The bands are assigned by taking into account the content, the language style, the layout and phonics. Word, phrase and sentence level work is also taken into consideration.

Maverick Early Readers are a bright, attractive range of books covering the pink to white bands. All of these books have been book banded for guided reading to the industry standard and edited by a leading educational consultant.

Pink
Red
Yellow
Blue
Green
Orange
Turquoise
Purple
Gold
White

To view the whole Maverick Readers scheme, visit our website at

www.maverickearlyreaders.com

Or scan the QR code above to view our scheme instantly!